MW00955900

THE BRIARPINS by **TOM WILSON.** Published by
AMAZON KDP PUBLISHING

No part of this publication may be reproduced in whole or in
Part, or stored in a retrieval system, or transmitted in any form or by
any means, electronic, mechanical, photocopying, recording, or otherwise,
without the written consent of the publisher/author. For information regarding permission,
write to **BRIARPINS@GMAIL.COM**

ISBN-13: 978-1-7353376-0-9

Text & illustration copyright © **2019** by **TOM WILSON**
Cover by **NICOLE PETROVSKY**

All rights reserved.

Published in the U.S.A.

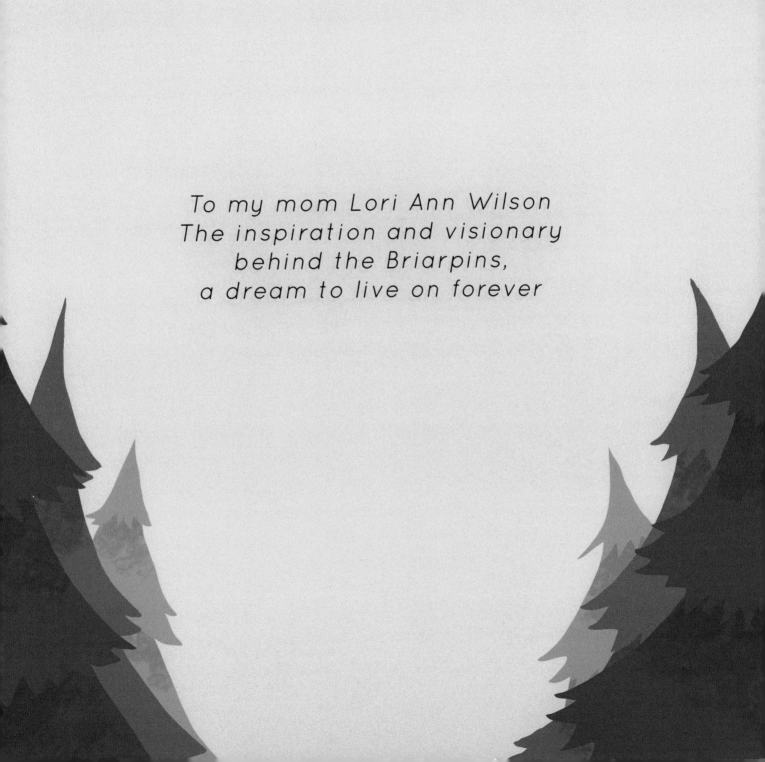

To my mom Lori Ann Wilson
The inspiration and visionary
behind the Briarpins,
a dream to live on forever

"Oakley...Oakley...where are you, boy?" called out Jack.

"Why do you run off, Oakley? Why are you so quick to leave?"

Jack checked for Oakley in the front yard...

the back yard...

and even down his boulevard.

He looked in all the spots Oakley was known to hide.

After much searching, Oakley was nowhere to be found, and Jack began to worry about where he may be.

Just as Jack's fears began to grow more and more...

"There you are, boy!" screamed Jack as Oakley ran toward him. Oakley jumped into Jack's outstretched arms and tackled him to the ground. "I thought we lost you, boy!" said Jack.

"So glad you found your way back home!" Jack always worried about Oakley, since Oakley was known to wander off without any warning.

After their long day of running around, Jack and Oakley were ready for bed. "Come on boy," called out Jack. Oakley jumped up on Jack's bed and curled into a ball next to Jack's feet.

"Love you, boy," said Jack, and he turned out the lights so they could fall asleep.

Jack and Oakley were sleeping soundly through the night, until...

"*Oakley...Oakley...where are you, boy?*" screamed Jack. At that moment, Jack realized he made a mistake. Jack forgot to close his bedroom door when they went to sleep. Oakley was not at his feet, and Jack presumed Oakley had run off.

Jack was so scared
Oakley left that he was
determined to find him.
Jack grabbed his flashlight
and his sweater, and put on
his favorite shoes to begin
his journey to find Oakley.

As Jack approached the kitchen, he noticed the backdoor was open. "Oh no!" said Jack.

"Mom asked me to close the door last night and I forgot. What a terrible mistake I have made." Jack became even more worried as he feared Oakley had gone outside.

Jack stood in the doorway and gazed into the distance. Jack then heard a noise near the forest.

Bark...Bark...Bark... "Oakley?!" yelled Jack. "I hear you, boy! I am on my way!" Jack switched on his flashlight and began the walk towards the forest.

Bark...bark...bark... Jack followed Oakley's sound and continued to call out.

"Oakley...Oakley...where are you, boy?" Jack got closer as Oakley's barks became louder and louder.

Jack could now hear Oakley through the bushes. However, Jack noticed something very odd...Oakley was playing with something Jack had never seen before.

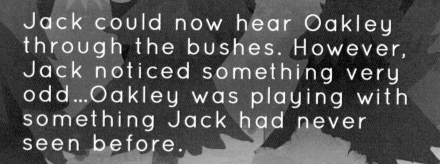

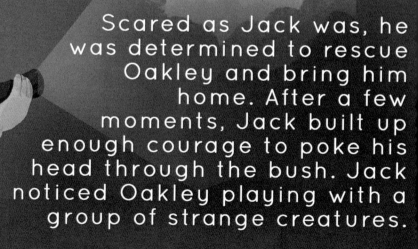

Scared as Jack was, he was determined to rescue Oakley and bring him home. After a few moments, Jack built up enough courage to poke his head through the bush. Jack noticed Oakley playing with a group of strange creatures.

"OAKLEY!" screamed Jack. The creatures became startled as they all looked back at Jack poking through the bush.

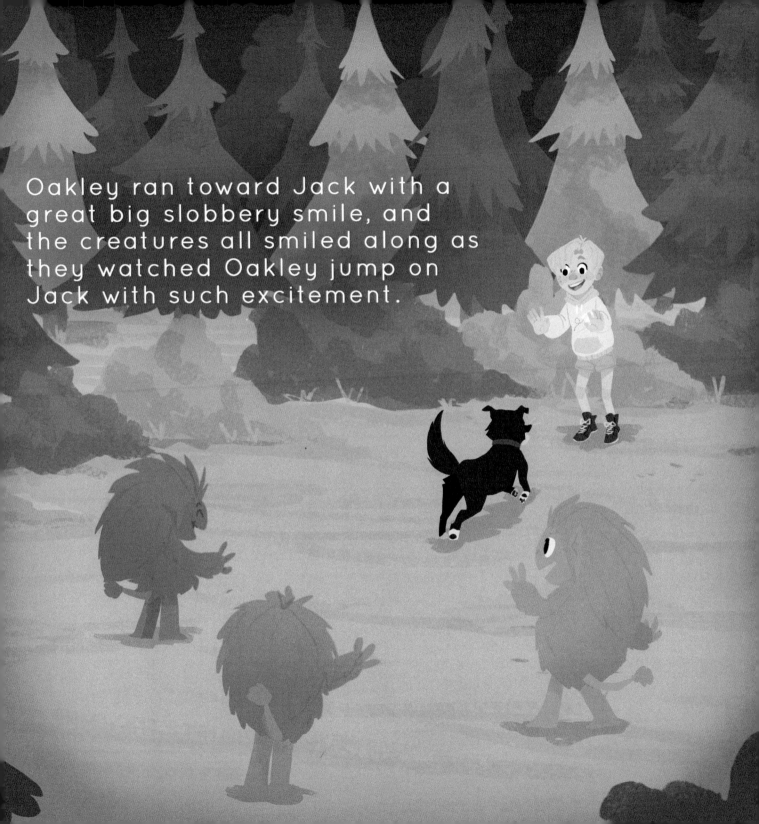

Oakley ran toward Jack with a great big slobbery smile, and the creatures all smiled along as they watched Oakley jump on Jack with such excitement.

"Hi Jack," said the creatures. "We are so glad to see you. We found Oakley out wandering through the forest. He was so scared when we discovered him."

"Thank you for finding Oakley for me. But who are you?" asked Jack.

"We are the Briarpins, Jack. We noticed Oakley out here and wanted to keep him safe until you found him. We are the ones who help Oakley find his way back home each time he gets lost. We love Oakley just as much as you do, but we think this is a good time to tell you something..."

"We know Oakley got out because the door was left open. It is okay to make mistakes, Jack. We all make mistakes. However, we are here to remind you that a lesson learned will live on forever, and we hope you learn from this mistake for your future."

"We Briarpins have seen people make many mistakes, but we have also seen the learning that takes place after their mistakes. A mistake does not define you, Jack. Mistakes can make you better going forward, but it is up to you whether you decide to learn from a mistake."

"I understand," stated Jack. "I have learned a great deal from my mistake tonight. I was so worried for Oakley. I will learn from this mistake and be sure to always shut my door before falling asleep."

"That's great!" said the Briarpins. "We are so glad to hear that. Now, what do you say we have some fun and hop through the forest on our journey back home?"

"That sounds fun!" said Jack. "Let's do it!"

Jack, Oakley and the Briarpins laughed and giggled as they hopped through the forest, jumping over each log, rock and stream they came across.

The Briarpins led Jack and Oakley to the edge of the forest, and they all waved goodbye. "Thank you again, Briarpins," said Jack. "Thank you for the valuable lesson I learned tonight. It was great to meet you, and hopefully we can see each other again soon."

Jack and Oakley went back to bed. Jack made sure to check the door was shut. "Love you, boy," said Jack, and gave Oakley a great big hug.

When Jack and Oakley fell asleep that night, they dreamed about their new-found friends and the marvelous lesson taught by the Briarpins.